Holy Spirit

By REV. LAWRENCE G. LOVASIK, S.V.D.
Divine Word Missionary

NIHIL OBSTAT: Daniel V. Flynn, J.C.D., *Censor Librorum*
IMPRIMATUR: ✠ Joseph T. O'Keefe, *Vicar General, Archdiocese of New York*

©1982 by *Catholic Book Publishing Corp., N.Y.*—Printed in China

ISBN 978-0-89942-310-4
CPSIA   December 2020   10 9 8 7 6 5 4 3   L/P

The Holy Trinity

JESUS taught us that the mystery of the Holy Trinity is the one true God in three Persons—the Father, the Son, and the Holy Spirit, and that each person is equal to each other.

Jesus made this mystery known to us because He wants us to know God as He is that we might love Him more in return for His love for us.

Jesus made the third Divine Person, the Holy Spirit, known to us. The Father and He, as the Risen Lord, sent the Holy Spirit to the Church.

The Holy Spirit is God, the Third Person of the Holy Trinity. He is really God, the same as the Father and the Son are really God. He is the Love of the Father and the Son.

Jesus Conceived by the Holy Spirit

THE angel Gabriel was sent from God to Nazareth, to the virgin Mary and said to her: "Hail Mary, full of grace! The Lord is with you. Blessed are you among women." Mary wondered what this greeting meant. The Angel went on to say to her: "Mary, do not be afraid. You have found favor with God. You shall conceive and bear a Son and give Him the Name Jesus. He will be called Son of the Most High."

Mary said to the Angel: "How can this be since I do not know man?"

The Angel answered her: "The Holy Spirit will come upon you and the power of the Most High will overshadow you. So the Child will be holy and will be called Son of God."

Mary said: "I am the servant of the Lord. Let it be done to me as you say." With that the Angel left her.

The greatest of God's works is the taking on of human flesh by His Son, Jesus Christ, and this is called the Incarnation. This was the work of the Holy Spirit because He is the Spirit of Love. Mary was the mother of Jesus. He was conceived by the Holy Spirit within her.

The Holy Spirit Comes Upon Jesus

JOHN the Baptist appeared in the desert, baptizing people and preaching his message. "Turn away from your sins and be baptized," he told the people, "and God will forgive your sins. The One who will come after me is much greater than I am; I am not worthy enough to bend down and untie His sandals. I baptize you with water, but He will baptize you with the Holy Spirit."

Not long afterward Jesus came from Nazareth and John baptized Him in the Jordan. As soon as Jesus came up out of the water He saw heaven opening and the Spirit coming down on Him like a dove. And a voice came from heaven: "You are My Son, the Beloved; My favor rests on You."

At once the Spirit made Him go into the desert.

This baptism was only a sign of penance. The Holy Spirit came down on Jesus like a dove. That is the reason why the Holy Spirit is represented by the dove, reminding us that He comes into our soul with His grace. He comes to us for the first time in the Sacrament of Baptism. The Holy Spirit comes to us in a special way in the Sacrament of Confirmation.

Jesus Preaches in the Holy Spirit

JESUS was always guided by the Holy Spirit. After His baptism of penance the Holy Spirit made Him go into the desert. Now He came to His own town, Nazareth, where He had grown up.

On the Sabbath day Jesus went as usual to the synagogue and stood up to read to the people. He read the prophecy of Isaiah: "The Spirit of the Lord has been given to Me, for He has anointed Me. He has sent Me to bring the Good News to the poor, to proclaim liberty to captives and to give the blind new sight, to set the downtrodden free and to proclaim the Lord's year of favor."

Jesus then said to the people: "This text is being fulfilled today even as you listen."

By this He meant that the Holy Spirit was with Him because He was the One Whom God had appointed to preach the Gospel to the poor and to preach the coming of the Lord.

9

Jesus Promises the Holy Spirit

AT the Last Supper Jesus spoke of the Holy Spirit and the work He would do in His Church. He promised to send a third Divine Person, the equal of Himself and the Father.

"I will ask the Father and He will give you another Paraclete, to be with you always: the Spirit of truth, Whom the world cannot accept, since it neither sees Him nor recognizes Him; but you can recognize Him because He remains with you and will be within you.

"This much have I told you while I was still with you; the Paraclete, the Holy Spirit Whom the Father will send in My Name, will instruct you in everything, and remind you of all that I told you.

"It is much better for you that I go. If I fail to go, the Paraclete will never come to you, whereas if I go, I will send Him to you. When He comes, being the Spirit of truth, He will guide you to all truth. In doing this He will give glory to Me, because He will have received from Me what He will announce to you."

The Holy Spirit is the Spirit of Truth because He reveals to the world the truth about the Father. The Holy Spirit is the Teacher Who will preserve the Church from error and keep it ever close to the mind of Christ. In this way, the Holy Spirit is to bear witness to Christ. The world will be informed about Christ through the Church, and the Holy Spirit is the soul of the Church.

Jesus Gives the Holy Spirit to the Apostles

IT was late that Sunday evening, the day on which Jesus rose from the dead. The Apostles were gathered behind locked doors for fear of the Jews. Jesus came and stood before them. "Peace be with you," He said. He showed them His hands and His side. At the sight of the Lord the disciples rejoiced.

"Peace be with you," He said again. "As the Father has sent Me, so I send you."

Then He breathed on them and said: "Receive the Holy Spirit. If you forgive men's sins, they are forgiven them; if you hold them bound, they are held bound."

The gift of the Holy Spirit, which can not be seen, flows from the risen Jesus. The Holy Spirit is God's Love.

The Holy Spirit takes away sin and gives us His peace because He helps us to return to God after we offended Him and unites us with Him by love through His grace.

Jesus gave His Apostles His Holy Spirit before giving them the power to forgive sins and giving us the Sacrament of Penance.

The Holy Spirit Comes to the Church

BEFORE Jesus ascended into heaven he said to His Apostles: "You will be filled with power when the Holy Spirit comes on you, and you will be witnesses for Me in Jerusalem and to the ends of the earth. Do not leave Jerusalem, but wait for the gift My Father promised, that I told you about. John baptized in water, but in a few days you will be baptized with the Holy Spirit."

When the day of Pentecost arrived, fifty days after Easter, all the believers were gathered together in one place. Suddenly there was a noise from the sky which sounded like a strong wind blowing, and it filled the whole house where they were sitting.

Then they saw what looked like tongues of fire spreading out, and each person there was touched by a tongue. They were all filled with the Holy Spirit and began to talk in other languages, as the Spirit enabled them to speak.

The Holy Spirit carried out the work of Jesus Christ on earth. That work is the salvation of all people. He spreads the Church throughout the world among people who are willing to love God and one another.

St. Peter's Sermon about the Holy Spirit

ON Pentecost day Peter stood up with the other eleven Apostles, and in a loud voice spoke to the crowd: "The Prophet Joel said, 'I will pour out My Spirit upon all people.' Jesus died and was buried. God has raised Him from the dead, and we are all witnesses to this fact.

"Jesus has been raised to the right hand of God and received from Him the Holy Spirit, as His Father had promised. What you now see and hear is His gift that He has poured out on us.

"Turn away from your sins and be baptized in the Name of Jesus Christ, so that your sins will be forgiven, and you will receive God's gift, the Holy Spirit. It was to you and your children that the promise was made, and to all those still far off whom the Lord our God calls."

Those who accepted this message were baptized. Some three thousand people were added to the Church that day.

The Holy Spirit in the Church

THE Church is the community of those who believe in Christ as Lord. The crucified and risen Jesus leads people to the Father by sending the Holy Spirit upon them.

At Pentecost the Holy Spirit came to remain with the Church forever. The Church was publicly made known to the people. The Gospel began to spread among the nations.

Today the Holy Spirit makes the Church grow. Through Him the Church is able to carry on the work of salvation given to it by Jesus Christ.

The Holy Spirit guides the Pope, bishops, and priests of the Catholic Church in their work of teaching Christ's doctrine, guiding souls and giving God's grace to the people through the Sacraments.

He directs all the work of Christ in the Church—the care of the sick, the teaching of children, the guidance of youth, the comforting of the sorrowful, the support of the needy.

The Holy Spirit guides the People of God in knowing the truth. He prays in them and makes them remember that they are adopted children of God. He brings the Church together in love and worship.

The Holy Spirit Comes to Us in Baptism and Confirmation

BAPTISM is a new birth as a child of God, a beginning of a new life in us of Jesus. Jesus Himself baptizes and makes us holy with the gifts of the Holy Spirit.

The Holy Spirit comes to us in a special way in the Sacrament of **Confirmation.** Confirmation is the Sacrament by which those who have been born again in Baptism now receive the seal of the Holy Spirit, the gift of the Father and the Son.

Confirmation unites us more perfectly to the Church and gives us the special strength of the Holy Spirit. This strength helps us to live in the world as a witness of Christ and to serve people.

The strength of the Holy Spirit will help us to bring Jesus Christ, His example, His way of life, and His Church, to others. But we must ask for this grace of the Holy Spirit often in prayer.

The Holy Spirit Gives Us Grace

THE Holy Spirit lives in our soul. He makes us holy by giving us **sanctifying grace,** God's own life in us, and by giving us the virtues of faith, hope, and love that come with it.

The Holy Spirit gives us the virtue of **faith** by helping us to believe God's word and to know that God loves us and cares for us and that we can trust Him.

The Holy Spirit gives us the virtue of **hope,** because in Jesus Christ God has promised us His love and care forever and will never leave us if only we remain united with Him.

The Holy Spirit gives us the virtue of **love,** the love of God and people, because they too belong to God. The presence of the Holy Spirit in us means that we are able to love with the love of God, even our enemies, if we want to do so.

The Holy Spirit also gives us **actual grace,** the help we need for mind and will to be good. It is special help which gives light to our mind and strength to our will to do good and to avoid evil.

The Holy Spirit unites us with God by love and helps us to keep our friendship with Him by prayer. He makes our prayer more pleasing to God through His grace.

The Holy Spirit
Lives in Our Soul

ST. Paul tells Christians that they are the temple of God. "Are you not aware that you are the temple of God, and that the Spirit of God dwells in you?"

Grace is God's gift of Himself. By grace we are united to the Father and to the Son in a union of love. We are also united to the Holy Spirit. Jesus said: "Anyone who loves me will be true to My word, and My Father will love Him; we will come to Him and make our dwelling place with Him."

United in Jesus as His followers, we are led by the Holy Spirit on our journey to the Kingdom of our heavenly Father. He helps us to fulfill our duties. He helps us to strive for what is good. He encourages us to pray. His grace unites us to the Most Holy Trinity by love.

St. Paul and the Holy Spirit

ST. Paul preached and wrote about the Holy Spirit. He said to the Galatians: "Let the Spirit direct your lives. The Spirit has given us life; He must also control our lives. The Spirit produces love, joy, peace, patience, kindness, goodness, faithfulness, humility, and self-control."

To the Ephesians, St. Paul said: "Do not make God's Holy Spirit sad. Do your best to preserve the unity which the Spirit gives, by the peace that binds you together. There is one body and one Spirit. I ask God to give you power through His Spirit to be strong in your inner selves, and that Christ will make His home in your hearts through faith."

To the Romans, St. Paul wrote: "Those who live as the Spirit tells them to, have their minds controlled by what the Spirit wants. This results in life and peace. Whoever does not have the Spirit of Christ does not belong to Him. If the Spirit of God, Who raised Jesus from death, lives in you, then He will also give life to your mortal bodies by the presence of His Spirit in you. Those who are led by God's Spirit are God's children. By the Spirit's power we cry to God, 'Father, my Father.' "

What We Believe about the Holy Spirit

W E can publicly declare our faith in the Holy Spirit by proclaiming a creed handed down from the early Church.

"I believe in one God,
the Father Almighty....

"I believe in one Lord Jesus Christ,
the Only Begotten Son of God....

For us men and for our salvation He came down from heaven,
and by the Holy Spirit was incarnate
    of the Virgin Mary,
and became man....
"I believe in the Holy Spirit, the Lord,
    the giver of life,
Who proceeds from the Father and the Son,
Who with the Father and the Son is adored and
    glorified,
Who has spoken through the Prophets."

How We Honor the Holy Spirit

WE should honor the Holy Spirit by loving Him as our God as we honor the Father and the Son. We should remember that He lives in our soul as in a temple.

We should honor the Holy Spirit by letting Him guide us in life. Since the Holy Spirit is always with us if we are in the state of grace, we should often ask Him for the light and strength we need to live a holy life and to save our soul.

We should ask Him to help us live as good Catholics according to the Gospel of Jesus Christ and the teaching of His Church.

We should ask Him to help the Holy Father, our bishops and priests and missionaries, that they may spread the Gospel of Jesus and bring souls to God.

We should ask Him to help our own family that we may live in love and peace and lead a good Christian life as Catholics should, so that we may be united with God in heaven after our death.

For the Seven Gifts
of the Holy Spirit

SPIRIT of **WISDOM**,
help me seek God.
Make Him the center of my life.
Make my life pleasing to Him,
so that love and peace
will always be in my soul.

    Spirit of **UNDERSTANDING**,
give light to my mind,
that I may know and love the truths of faith
and make them truly my own.

Spirit of **COUNSEL**,
give me light and guide me
    in all my ways,
that I may always know and do Your holy will.

Spirit of **FORTITUDE**,
give strength to my soul
in every time of trouble or danger.
Let me never offend God by willful sin.
Strengthen me against temptation.

Spirit of **KNOWLEDGE**,
help me to know good from evil.
Teach me to do what is right
in the sight of God.

Spirit of **PIETY**,
live in my heart,
draw it to true faith in You,
to a holy love of You, my God.
Make me seek You with my whole soul,
and find You, my best and truest Friend.

Spirit of **HOLY FEAR**,
make me always remember Your presence
    in my soul.
Keep me from sin and give me great
    reverence for God and for all people.

Consecration to the Holy Spirit

G OD Holy Spirit,
  You are the Infinite Love
of the Father and the Son.

Through the pure hands of Mary,
Your Immaculate Bride,
I place myself this day,
and all the days of my life,
upon Your chosen altar,
the Divine Heart of Jesus,
as an offering to You, consuming Fire.

May I ever hear Your voice,
and do in all things
Your most Holy and Adorable Will.

God, Holy Spirit, I love You.